THE
BLUE
RIBBON
PUPPIES
by
CROCKETT
JOHNSON

ISBN 0-590-43630-9

12 11 10 9 8 7 6 5 4 3   4 5/9

Printed in the U.S.A.   08

There were seven pups, and the
children said, "We will put a blue
ribbon on the BEST puppy here."
They tried a ribbon on one pup.
"He is too fat," said the boy.

The puppy looked at him.
"He's the best," the boy said,
"the best FAT puppy."

The children let the fat pup keep
his blue ribbon and they got another
ribbon to try on another puppy.
"He is too spotty," said the girl.

7

The puppy looked at her.
"He's the best," the girl said,
"the best SPOTTY puppy."

9

So the spotty pup kept his ribbon
and the children got another ribbon
for the next pup.

"He is too long," said the boy.

11

The puppy looked at him.
"He's the best," the boy said,
"the best LONG puppy."

The three pups with blue ribbons
watched the children try a new blue
ribbon on another pup.

"He is too tall," said the girl.

The puppy looked at her.
"He's the best," the girl said,
"the best TALL puppy."

The children put another ribbon
on another pup.
"He is too small," said the boy.

19

The puppy looked at him.
"He's the best," the boy said,
"the best SMALL puppy."

Wearing his blue ribbon the small
puppy joined the others as the boy
put a ribbon on another pup.

"He is too shaggy," said the girl.

23

The puppy looked at her.
"He is the best," the girl said,
"the best SHAGGY puppy."

25

There was one puppy left and the
children put a ribbon on him.
"He is not fat, spotty, long, tall,
small or shaggy," said the boy.
"He is too plain," said the girl.

The puppy looked at the children.
"He's the best," they said, "the
best PLAIN puppy."

The boy and girl patted each
of the pups and congratulated
them.   And the pups, wearing